For Everyone to Share

For Amy, Daniel and Kate
G.L.

For my beautiful daughter Chloe
D.H.

Copyright © 2008 by Good Books, Intercourse, PA 17534
International Standard Book Number: 978-1-56148-598-7
Library of Congress Catalog Card Number: 2007009592

Text © Gillian Lobel 2007
Illustrations © Daniel Howarth 2007

Original edition published in Great Britain in 2007 by Gullane Children's Books,
an imprint of Alligator Books Ltd, Winchester House,
259-269 Old Marylebone Road,
London NW1 5XJ, England.

Printed in China

Library of Congress Cataloging-in-Publication Data

Lobel, Gillian.
For everyone to share / Gillian Lobel & [illustrations by] Daniel Howarth.
p. cm.
Summary: When Little Mouse ventures out of his nest for the first
time, he finds a world of beauty and wonders, which his mother assures
him is for everyone to share.
ISBN-13: 978-1-56148-598-7 (hardcover)
[1. Nature--Fiction. 2. Mice--Fiction.] I. Howarth, Daniel, ill. II. Title.
PZ7.L7798For 2008
[E]--dc22
2007009592

For Everyone to Share

Gillian Lobel • Daniel Howarth

Intercourse, PA 17534
800/762-7171
www.GoodBooks.com

Little Mouse was fast asleep in his soft, cozy nest.
He was so warm, snuggled next to his mother and his six
brothers and sisters. Suddenly his nose tickled . . .
"Achoo!" said Little Mouse.

He did a big stretch, from his tiny pink nose,
to his long curly tail. Little Mouse scrambled out
of his nest. All around him it was dark and dim.
But far away, he saw something different.
Something that made his eyes
water for a moment.

What was it?

Little Mouse pattered along
a leafy tunnel. Strange
smells tickled his nose. His
whiskers quivered with excitement.

And suddenly he was there – there in the big brightness.

Curiously he tiptoed into the daylight . . .

And he saw — a tiny fat person, dressed in a furry coat
of black and gold! He zizzed loudly in Little Mouse's ears.
"Who are you?" cried Little Mouse. "Please tell me your name!"
The furry person zizzed even louder.
"I'm a **bee**, Little Mouse!"
And he flew away and . . .

landed on something yellow and shining.
"Don't go," squeaked Little Mouse.
"Please tell me what you're sitting on!"

"This is a **flower**, Little Mouse," zizzed the bee.
And he climbed right into the heart of the flower to sip his breakfast.
"Bee, flower," murmured Little Mouse. "What a wonderful place this is!"

He felt something soft on his back, and he
lifted his eyes. Far, far above him was a glowing ring
of light! It shone on his ears and toes and warmed them.
"Please tell me, Buzzy Bee, who is that?"
Little Mouse pointed high into the sky.

"That's the **sun**, Little Mouse –
the blessed sun! And she lives in the **bright blue sky**."
"Bee, flower, sun and **bright blue sky**," murmured Little
Mouse. "And what is that, Buzzy Bee? Please tell me."

But Buzzy Bee had zizzed away.

Just then, something floated past Little Mouse's nose and landed right next to him. She was as blue as the sky and lighter than the air. "Oh Little Sky," he gasped. "Please tell me who you are." "I am a **butterfly**, Little Mouse," she breathed, and a silvery laugh rippled over the flowers.

"Bee, flower, sun, sky and butterfly," murmured Little Mouse. "How wonderful this place is!"

"And there is even more," said the butterfly. "Look!"
And she showed him the birds, who filled the air with music, the
whispering grasses, starry daisies, and the dewdrops on a spider's web.

"And now I must go," said the blue butterfly.
"Goodbye, Little Mouse!" And up and away she fluttered.

Little Mouse trembled with excitement.
"I will go home and tell everyone what I have seen!"

But Mommy Mouse was already out looking for him.

"Mommy, Mommy!" called Little Mouse joyfully. "I have seen so
many things here in the big outside – a buzzy bee, a flower,
the golden sun, the bright blue sky, a butterfly,
the birds of the air – oh, so much.
What is this place, Mommy? Please
tell me. I want to know!"

"Why, this is the **world**,
Little Mouse – the beautiful
world!" laughed his mother.

And they trotted home
happily together.

"The world . . . ," murmured Little Mouse as he
snuggled into his mother's arms. "The big, beautiful world.
But who is it for, Mommy? Is it a world for us?"

"Yes," smiled his mother. "It is a world for bees and butterflies
and flowers, for birds and spiders and grasses that sing.
And it's a world for us, too – it's a world . . .

for everyone to share!"

Little Mouse gave a deep and happy sigh.
He curled into his sweet, warm nest
with his six brothers and sisters
and fell fast asleep.